Dear Bear

by Joanna Harrison

Carolrhoda Books, Inc./Minneapolis

For James,
Katie
and Hugo.
x x x

Copyright © 1994 by Joanna Harrison

With special thanks to my daughter Katie, aged six, for
writing and illustrating Katie's letters to the bear.

This edition first published in 1994 by Carolrhoda Books, Inc.

First published in England in 1994 by HarperCollins Publishers Ltd, London.
All rights to this edition reserved by Carolrhoda Books,
Inc. No part of this book may be reproduced, stored in a
retrieval system, or transmitted in any form or by any
means, electronic, mechanical, photocopying, recording, or
otherwise, without the prior written permission of
Carolrhoda Books, Inc. except for the inclusion of brief
quotations in an acknowledged review.

This book is available in two editions:
Library binding by Carolrhoda Books, Inc.
Soft cover by First Avenue Editions
c/o The Lerner Group
241 First Avenue North
Minneapolis, Minnesota 55401

LIBRARY OF CONGRESS CATALOGING-IN-PUBLICATION DATA

Harrison, Joanna
    Dear Bear / by Joanna Harrison.
        p. cm.
        Summary: Katie is afraid of the bear that lives under the stairs in her house,
until they exchange letters and she finally gets to meet him.
        ISBN 0-87614-839-9 (lib.bdg.)
        ISBN 0-87614-965-4 (pbk.)
        [I. Teddy Bears—Fiction. 2. Letters—Fiction. 3. Fear—Fiction.] 1. Title
PZ7.H252De 1994
[E]—dc20   93-44730
                                                                      CIP
                                                                       AC

Printed in Hong Kong
Bound in the United States of America
3 4 5 6 - 0S - 99 98 97 96

Katie liked having tea parties. It meant she didn't have to think about the bear.

Well, the bear didn't worry her that much. After all, it didn't bother her when she was busy at home...

...and she could even laugh about it at school.

But when she was at home in bed, however hard she tried, she couldn't stop thinking about the bear who lived under the stairs. She had never seen him, but she knew he was there, just waiting to jump out and grab her.

Sometimes huge bear-like shadows would chase her up the stairs. Katie decided to tell her parents about it.

She tried her dad, but he was
too busy vacuuming.

Her mom said, "Why don't you write the bear a letter and
tell him to go away?"

So Katie took out her pencils and paper and wrote the bear a letter.

She put it in an envelope

and left it outside the closet door.

This is what it said:

The next morning, the letter was gone. In its place was another one. It was addressed to Katie. It read:

UNDER THE STAIRS

DEAR KATIE,
            I HAVE
TAKEN YOUR ADVICE
AND GONE AWAY.
     I AM MUCH IN NEED
OF A VACATION FROM
SITTING IN THE CLOSET
ALL DAY
            LOVE FROM
            BEAR xx

P.S. BACK MONDAY.

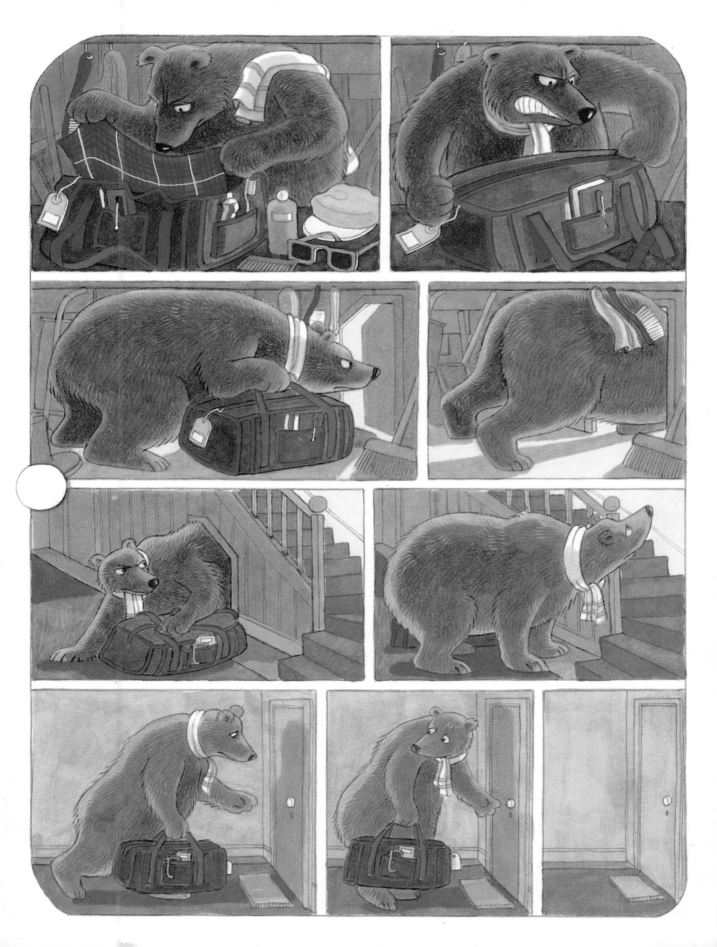

During the next few days

Katie couldn't stop thinking...

...about the bear

on vacation.

But when Monday came, Katie didn't want to come home from school.

When she arrived home, she found a package in front of the closet door. Katie opened it up.

Inside was a little glass dome filled with snow.

With it was this card:

DEAR KATIE,
JUST A LITTLE
PRESENT I BOUGHT
FOR YOU WHILE
I WAS ON VACATION
LOVE FROM
BEAR XX
P.S. IT'S NICE TO BE BACK.

Katie showed her dad. "How
generous," he said. "Why don't you
write him a thank you letter?"

After Katie had written her letter, she put it in an envelope and dropped it over the banister.

It read:

Dear Bear Thankyou for my present. love from Katie x Here it is on my piano

There was no reply the next day...

or the day after...

or the day after that.

Katie started to worry about the bear, so she wrote him another letter. This is what it said:

Dear Bear
    why dont you
write to me any more.
Are you ill?
    love from
        Katie.

Katie

my cat

Bear

The next day, she received this reply:

DEAR KATIE. THANKYOU FOR YOUR LETTER. I HAVE HAD A VERY BAD COLD. PLEASE DONT WORRI. LOVE BEAR x

KATIE

Katie rushed to show her mom.

Her mom was very concerned.

"We'll make him a hot-water bottle,

some sandwiches,

and a nice cup of tea."

Katie knocked on the closet door. "Dear Bear," she whispered, "are you all right?" There was no answer.

The next morning the tray was gone. In its place was a letter.

UNDER THE STAIRS

DEAR KATIE,
            THANKYOU FOR
THE HOT-WATER BOTTLE AND
TEA. I AM NOW FEELING
MUCH BETTER.
      WOULD YOU LIKE TO
COME TO TEA WITH ME
TOMORROW AFTERNOON AT
ABOUT 4 o'CLOCK?
      LOVE FROM
         BEAR xx

Katie read the letter to her parents. "I see the Bears won again," said her father. He wasn't really listening.

Katie spent all the next afternoon getting ready

for her tea party with the bear. She put on her best outfit and

even brushed her hair.

But when four o'clock came, she wasn't so sure she wanted to go. After all, he was still the bear in the closet.

"Go on," said her mom, "he'll be expecting you."

And…

...he was.